THIS ZOO IS NOT FOR YOU

For Corra and Cairn—
this zoo is for you

First U.S. edition 2018

Library of Congress Catalog Card Number pending
ISBN 978-1-5362-0015-7

WKT 22 21 20 19 18 17
10 9 8 7 6 5 4 3 2 1

Printed in Shenzhen, Guangdong, China

This book was typeset in Miller Banner.
The illustrations were done using watercolor and charcoal.

Nosy Crow
an imprint of Candlewick Press,
99 Dover Street, Somerville, Massachusetts 02144

www.nosycrow.com
www.candlewick.com

nosy Crow
An imprint of Candlewick Press

ROSS COLLINS

THIS ZOO IS NOT FOR YOU

Hello, come in.
How do you do?
Have you come
for the interview?

A platypus!
That's strange and new!
You're meeting Panda first—
go through.

I'm special, rare,
and **famous**, too.

To get me here
was **quite** a coup.
But you don't even
eat **bamboo**!

I think this zoo
is **not** for you.

We're elegant and graceful, too.
We really do **enhance** the view.

But you look like
a **worn-out shoe.**

And so this zoo
is **not** for you.

We're **very** good at throwing poo.
Young Jeffrey here can play **kazoo**.

Is there a **trick** that you can do?
If not, this zoo
is **not** for you.

We are a multicolored crew.
We're **green**, then **red**,
then **pink** or **blue**.

Is brownish-gray
your **only** hue?

It's clear this zoo
is **not** for you.

I'm powerful
and **huge**, it's true.

You are short
and quite weird, too.

You've simply **failed**
this interview.

You see, this zoo
is **not** for you.

I'm not proud of that interview.
I think I was **unkind.** Were you?

Perhaps he **could** have
joined our zoo.

But now he's gone.
What **should** we do?

We **must** apologize to you.
You didn't **want** to
join our zoo.
We got it **wrong,**
that much is true.

We found your
invitation, too!

We'd **love** to still
be friends . . .

would you?

It's OK,
guys. . . .

This **platybus** is
for **all** of us!